Clifford's™ puppy days

BACKPACK PUPPY

By Sarah Fisch
Illustrated by Jim Durk

Based on the Scholastic book series "Clifford The Big Red Dog" by Norman Bridwell

ISBN 0-439-73379-0

10 9 8 7 6 5   09

Designed by Michael Massen

Printed in the U.S.A.   First printing, September 2005

SCHOLASTIC INC.

New York   Toronto   London   Auckland   Sydney
Mexico City   New Delhi   Hong Kong   Buenos Aires

On the last day of summer vacation, Nina and Jorgé visited Emily Elizabeth and Clifford.

"Are these your new supplies for tomorrow?" Nina asked.

"Yes," Emily Elizabeth answered. "I'm glad we'll be together for our first day of school!"

"What is school?" Clifford asked Jorgé.
"Nina and Emily Elizabeth will go to school every day," Jorgé replied. "They learn and play, and eat lunch in the cafeteria."

"Wow!" Clifford said. "I can't wait to go!"
Jorgé chuckled. "No, Clifford. We will stay home."
"Puppies don't belong at school," added Daffodil.

"We have fun right here!" Jorgé exclaimed. "We don't need to go to school."

Clifford wasn't so sure. Emily Elizabeth had never left him alone all day before!

"Hey, buddy," Norville joked to Clifford, "why don't you wear a backpack and disguise yourself as a kid?" The parrot laughed. "Then you can go to school, too." Norville wasn't serious—but he'd given the little red puppy a great big idea!

The next morning, Mr. Howard and Mr. Flores walked Emily Elizabeth and Nina to their first day of school.

"I'm so excited!" Nina said.
"Me too, but this backpack sure is heavy," Emily Elizabeth replied. "Maybe I brought too many supplies."

From his hiding place inside the backpack, Clifford heard, "Welcome, everybody! I'm your teacher, Ms. Parker!"

The teacher's voice was so friendly Clifford wanted to bark hello, but he didn't want to give himself away.

As Emily Elizabeth entered her new classroom, Clifford held his breath, wondering if he would be found.

Emily Elizabeth didn't notice him.

That was close! Clifford thought. He decided to take a look around.

EMILY ELIZAB

"Does everybody know the song 'Old McDonald Had a Farm'?" Ms. Parker asked.
"Yes!" the children shouted.

"Old McDonald had a farm," the children sang, "E-I-E-I-O! On that farm he had a—"

"Dog!" Ms. Parker sang.

"E-I-E-I-O!" the children continued.

Did she say "dog"? Clifford thought.

That was Clifford's favorite part of the song! No wonder Emily Elizabeth loved school.

"With a woof-woof here and a woof-woof there," the children sang. "Here a woof! There a woof! Everywhere a—"

"Woof-woof!" Clifford barked loudly.

"*Clifford!*" squeaked Emily Elizabeth.
"Emily Elizabeth Howard!" Ms. Parker gasped.
"Where did this little red puppy come from?"

"Clifford didn't mean to do anything wrong," Emily Elizabeth whispered.

"Maybe so," Ms. Parker replied sternly, "but puppies are not allowed in school."

"Since he's already here, Clifford can stay the morning," Ms. Parker told Emily Elizabeth. "Your mother will need to pick him up before lunch."

"Hooray!" the children cheered.

Emily Elizabeth promised that Clifford would behave himself.

Scritch scritch scritch—that was the noise Emily Elizabeth's pencil made as she pushed it on the paper.

That's a funny game! Clifford thought. He grabbed the pencil right out of Emily Elizabeth's hand, but she made him give it back.

"Clifford, sit still and be quiet, okay?" Emily Elizabeth asked. Clifford tried hard. He sat and he sat. He didn't make a sound. It was very difficult being still and quiet!

Clifford's tummy rumbled. It was past his lunchtime. He yawned. *At home, I'd be napping in my comfy bed now,* he thought. Maybe Daffodil was right—puppies didn't belong in school!

When Mrs. Howard came to pick up Clifford, he was ready to go. "Bye-bye, Clifford," Emily Elizabeth said. "See you at home!" *Home,* Clifford thought happily. *Now that's where puppies belong!*